PIC
Dunbar

PPP
$13.00
4/2010

For Katherine and Ant

First U.S. edition 2008

Library of Congress Cataloging-in-Publication Data is available.

Library of Congress Catalog Card Number 2007052884

ISBN 978-0-7636-4110-8

2 4 6 8 10 9 7 5 3 1

Printed in China

This book was typeset in Gill Sans MT Schoolbook.
The illustrations were done in mixed media.

Candlewick Press
2067 Massachusetts Avenue
Cambridge, Massachusetts 02140

visit us at www.candlewick.com

Tilly and
her friends
all live
together in
a little yellow
house....

Happy
Hector

Polly Dunbar

CANDLEWICK PRESS
CAMBRIDGE, MASSACHUSETTS

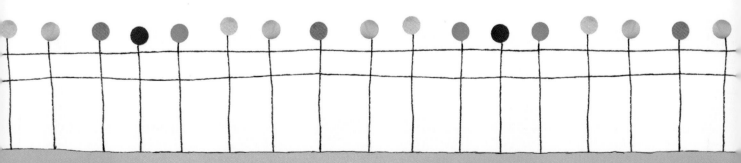

Hector
was sitting on
Tilly's lap.

"I am the

happiest

I have ever

been!"

he said.

Tumpty and Doodle were happy, too.

They were playing cars.

Pru was happily
combing her
feathers.

And Tiptoe was happily painting a
wonderful picture.

"Come and paint
with me!"
he said.

"No thanks," said Hector.
"We're **happy** sitting here."

But Tiptoe **really**
wanted to play with Tilly.

So he hopped onto Tilly's lap.

"Oh!" said Hector.

"Look at them having fun,"

said Doodle.

"Let's join in!"

"**Oh, no!**" said Hector.

Hector went off to be alone.

"Now I am the unhappiest I have ever been," he said.

"Will you play cars with me?"

asked Doodle.

"Can I comb your ears?"

asked Pru.

"Can I paint your nose blue?"
asked Tiptoe.

"NO, YOU CAN'T!"
said Hector.

"Can I sit on your lap?"

asked Tumpty.

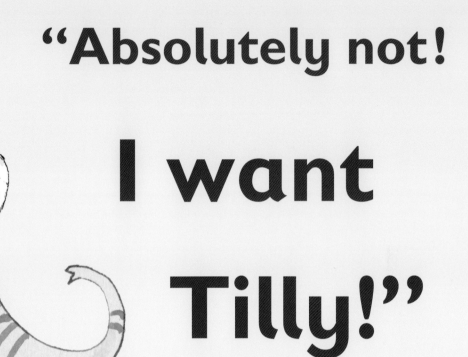

"Absolutely not!

I want

Tilly!"

cried Hector.

But Tilly was busy . . .

painting a wonderful picture . . .

of Hector!

"Wow!" said Hector.

Hector was happy.

So happy

that he even let Tiptoe

paint his nose

blue.

Then Hector sat
on Tilly's lap.

"Now," he said,

"I am the

happiest,

happiest

I have ever

been!"

The End